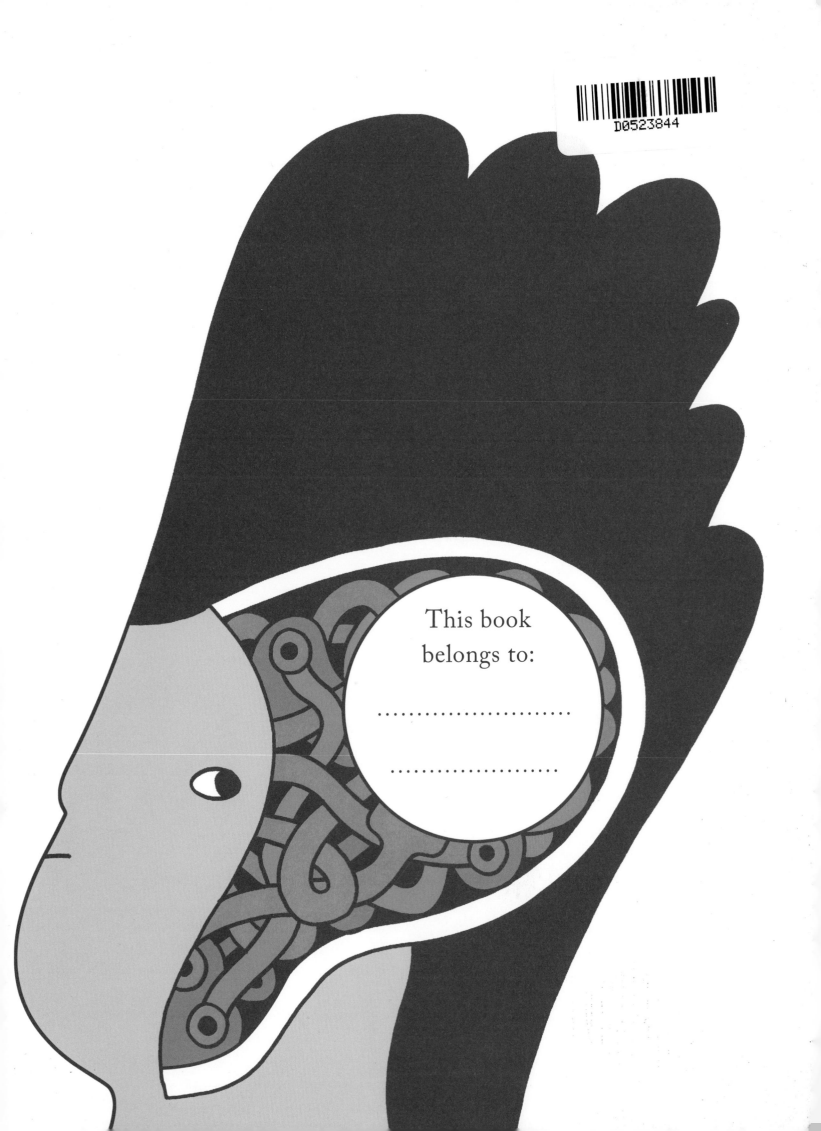

This book
belongs to:

....

....

To Indigo & Vincent

A TEMPLAR BOOK

First published in the UK in 2019 by Templar Books,
an imprint of Bonnier Books UK,
The Plaza, 535 King's Road, London, SW10 0SZ
www.templarco.co.uk
www.bonnierbooks.co.uk

Text copyright © 2019 by James Thorp
Illustration copyright © 2019 by Angus Mackinnon
Design copyright © 2019 by Templar Books
1 3 5 7 9 10 8 6 4 2

ISBN 978-1-78741-193-7

This book was typeset in Adobe Caslon Pro
The illustrations were drawn in pen and ink
and coloured digitally

Designed by Genevieve Webster
Edited by Katie Haworth
Production Controller: Sian Cheung

Printed in China

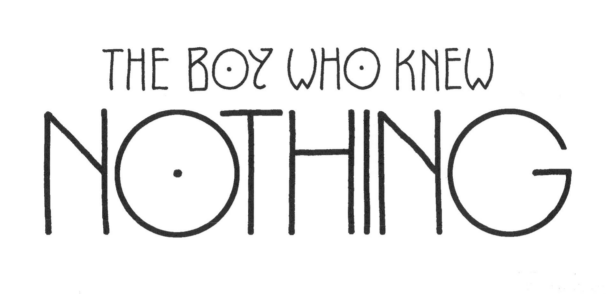

THE BOY WHO KNEW
NOTHING

JAMES
THORP

ANGUS
MACKINNON

templar
books

On the day he was born,
before he could crawl,
the boy who knew nothing
knew nothing at all.

No A's and no B's,
no twos and no threes,
no points of the compass
or words for the trees.

He lived on the island
of Solo Capoo,
in a broken-down house
with a wonderful view.

And he grew and he grew
and he went to the school,
where the children all pointed
and called him a fool.

One day, while his parents
were snoozing a snooze,
he went to their bedroom
to play in their shoes.

"Wow, what is this thingammy,
some kind of fox?"
said the boy pulling clothes
from a dressing-up box.

With the thing in his arms
he ran down the stairs,
to wake up his parents
asleep in their chairs.

"Hey what is this
thingy-macguffin?"he said.
"It looks like a snow fox,
but not quite as red."

"Oh don't be so daft,"
said his dad with a laugh.
"Everyone knows
that's a sleepy giraffe!"

Everyone knows?
Everyone knows?
Everyone knows that's a sleepy giraffe?

A sleepy giraffe
or a fox made of snow?
The boy who knew nothing
he wanted to know.

So . . .

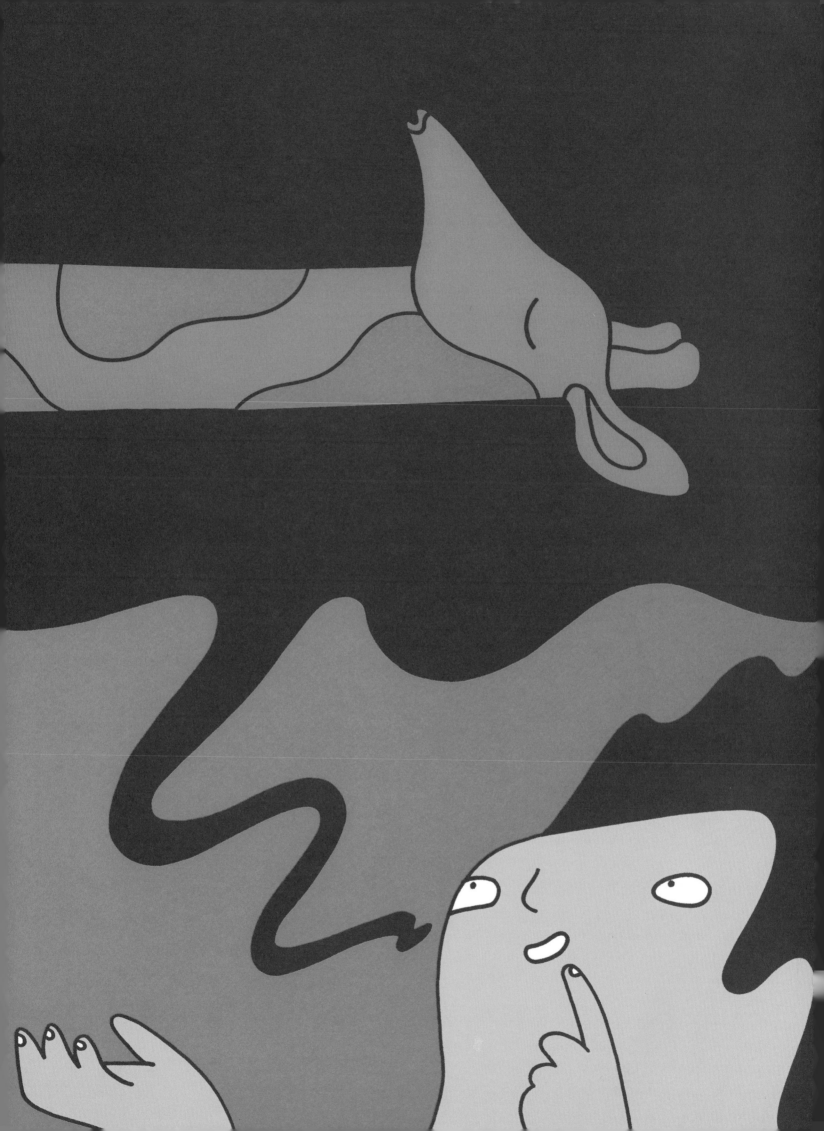

He rode on his bicycle
down to the quay,
to ask the old whispering witch
of the sea.

"Please what is this thingy I've found?"
asked the boy.
"A fox, a giraffe
or a new kind of toy?"

"Oh don't be a fool,"
said the witch with a scowl.
"Everyone knows
that's a whispery owl!"

Everyone knows?
Everyone knows?
Everyone knows that's a whispery owl?

"Not everyone knows,"
said the boy to himself.
"Yes, it could be an owl,
or it could be an elf.

"I need to find someone
who's clever," he thought.
"Like clumsy Miss Susan,
the ex-astronaut."

So . . .

He jumped on a train,
with the thing on his knee,
and rode to the roots
of the astronaut's tree.

"Excuse me, Miss Susan,
what is this please?
A sleepy giraffe?
Or an owl made of cheese?"

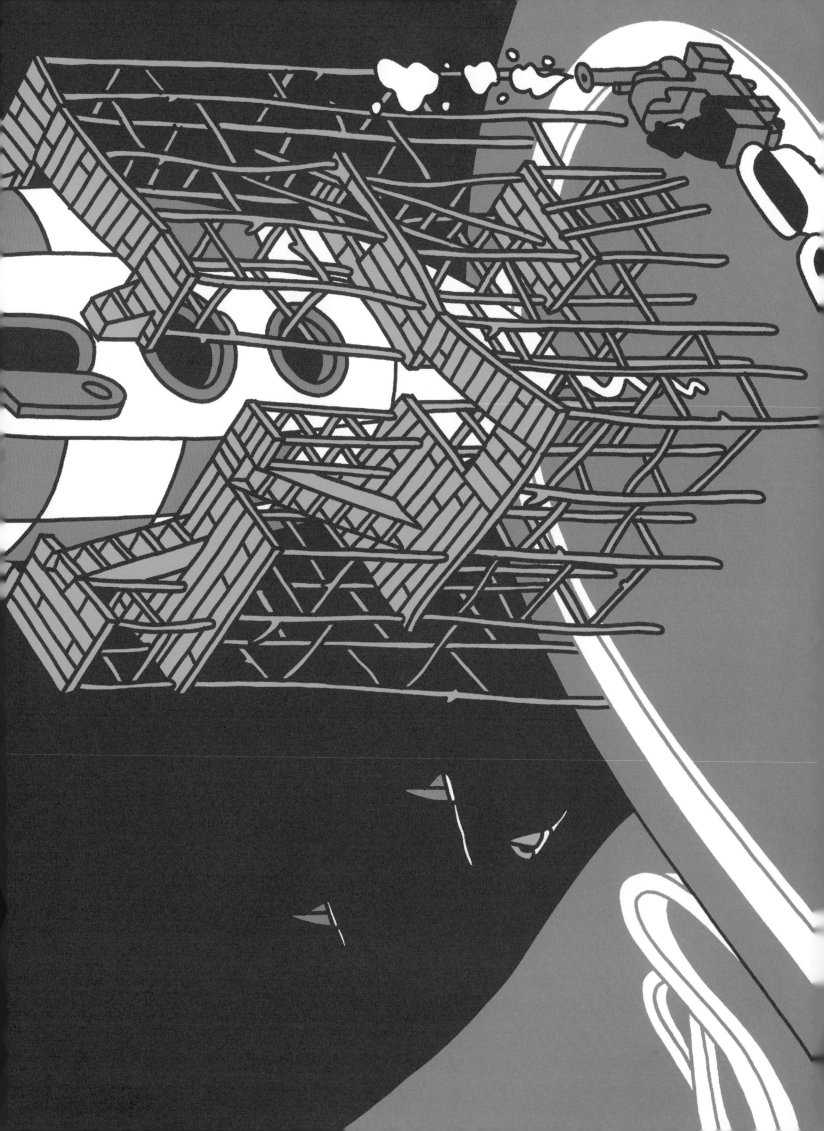

"Oh don't be so stupid."
She tripped on her shoe.
"Everyone knows
that's a clumsy gnu."

Everyone knows?
Everyone knows?
Everyone knows that's a clumsy gnu?

A clumsy G . . . No!

The boy held his hands up
and stared at the floor.
"Okay, that's enough,
I can't take any more."

He said to Miss Susan,
"I know what to do."
And off on the back of his thingy
he flew.

That night when the boy returned home
it was late.
His parents were waiting outside
by the gate.

"Just where have you been
in those trousers?" they said.
"And why have you got that
giraffe on your head?"

"It's not a giraffe, a gnu
or an owl,"
said the boy wiping mud
from his face with a towel.

"I went on a magic
adventure," he smiled.
"And spoke to the thingies
that live in the wild."

"I went to the zoo,
saw a gnu,
and now I know all the things
gnus like to do.

"I went for a prowl,
spotted an owl,
and now I know all the things
owls like to howl.

"And after his bath,
I met a giraffe,
who taught me to dance
in an hour and a half."

"Hmmm.
It sounds very tiring,"
his mum and dad said.
"So all of you, upstairs,
you're going to bed."

The boy said goodnight
to the witch and Miss Susan,
the owl and giraffe,
and the clumsy gnu and . . .

"Hey, where did my friend the
thingammy-thing go?"

"I'm here," said the thing,
and my name is . . .

Next morning the boy
took Flamingo to school,
and together they taught
all the children a rule:

If ever there's something
you don't understand,
don't be too frightened
to put up your hand.

For even your smartest,
most brilliant friend,
started out life
knowing nothing . . .

THE
END

Also by James Thorp & Angus Mackinnon:

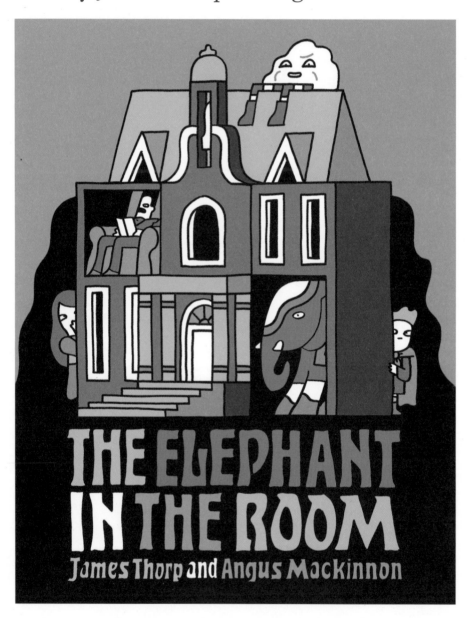

ISBN: 978-1-78370-773-7 (hardback)
978-1-78741-445-7 (paperback)